Red, Blue and Yellow Yarn

A Tale of Forgiveness

by Miriam R. Kosman
illustrated by Valeri Gorbachev

This **PJ BOOK** belongs to

_____

_____

PJ Library®

JEWISH BEDTIME STORIES and SONGS

BS"D

Red, Blue and Yellow Yarn

*To Lori Meresohn of Johannesburg, S. A., whose thirst for
knowledge, and courage and determination to grow, has
given us much joy, as well as something to emulate.
With love, The Kosman Family*

For my grandchildren: Faige, Yosef, and Yitzhak. V. G.

First Edition – September 1996 / Elul 5756
PJ Library Edition – April 2016 / Adar 2, 5776
Copyright © 1996 by HACHAI PUBLISHING
ALL RIGHTS RESERVED

ISBN: 978-0-922613-78-6 (Hardcover edition)
LCCN: 95-079439

HACHAI PUBLISHING
Brooklyn, New York
Tel: 718-633-0100 Fax: 718-633-0103
www.hachai.com - info@hachai.com

Printed in China

Bubby, Donny's grandmother, was here for a visit.
She was planning to stay for a whole week.

When Bubby came, she slept in Donny's room, and Donny had to sleep downstairs in the den. When Bubby was here, Donny had to walk on tip-toes while she rested.

He wasn't allowed to play ball on the wall of the house, because Bubby didn't like the noise.

Donny had to wash with soap and a nailbrush before every meal, because Bubby would inspect his hands. Bubby always ate with a napkin on her lap and insisted that Donny do the same.

It seemed like whenever Bubby was here, Donny got into trouble.

She had so many rules, and somehow, Donny always managed to break some. Sometimes, he wondered if Bubby even liked him.

Right now, Bubby was in the kitchen talking to Mommy. No one would hear him if he crept into his room to see if he had left his little blue car on the bed. Slowly and quietly, Donny opened the door. Then he just stopped and stared.

Donny's bed, the one Bubby was using now, was piled high with balls of yarn. Green and yellow, blue and pink. Grey yarn with flecks of black. Brown yarn with flecks of orange.

Donny forgot all about his car.

He forgot that he wasn't allowed
in Bubby's room. He didn't think about
what Mommy would say. He just couldn't
stop himself from squeezing one ball of yarn and throwing
it in the air. What a perfect size for juggling!

Donny tossed up a blue one and a green one. The blue
ball of yarn dropped and rolled into a corner, trailing a long
blue tail after it. Donny grabbed a yellow ball of yarn and
kept on juggling.

Red. Green. Yellow. Blue. Faster. Higher.
The balls flew up and down, in and out.

Suddenly, there were voices on the stairs. Mommy and Bubby were coming!

The door opened, and they both stood staring. Donny looked around the room. What a mess!

A carpet of colored yarn covered the floor. Strings of green
yarn and red yarn snaked around the legs of the bed. Long
strands of yellow yarn and blue yarn hung down from the dresser.
The room was covered, and the bed was empty.

"Donny," Mommy gasped. "What have you done?"

She tried to push the door open wider, but it got stuck on a clump of red, blue and yellow yarn.

"Donny," she said, "I expect you to wind up every one of these balls of yarn again. And don't come back downstairs until you are finished."

Slowly, Donny picked up the end of a red strand
and began to wind. He wound and wound until – oops!
He came to a tangle. The red yarn was twisted around
the blue.

Donny unraveled the knot and picked up two balls at
a time. He tried rolling them together, stepping over and
under each ball to get them straightened out.

Soon he sat down with a plop. So much yarn was tied and twisted around his pants. How was he ever going to finish this? Donny imagined himself as an old man, winding and winding away, his long white beard covered with blue and yellow yarn.

Donny started to cry.

All at once, the door opened, and Bubby walked in. Donny jumped up and quickly wiped his eyes. Had Bubby come to tell him how wrong it was to touch her things?

Bubby smiled. "Come, Donny," she said. "You look like you could use some help."

Donny couldn't believe it. Bubby didn't look a bit angry.

"Here," she said, untangling a blue strand from around Donny's leg and handing it to him. "You start winding this, and I'll work on the other end."

The work went much faster with Bubby's help. She and Donny walked around and around each other so that the yarn would unravel. Little by little, the room began to look neater.

Bubby sat down and took out a piece of cardboard. She wrapped some yarn around the cardboard, turning it to form a perfect ball. Donny sat down next to her.

"I'm sorry," he whispered.

Bubby turned and looked right at him.

"Donny," she said in a smiley voice, "let me tell you a story about when I was a little girl." Bubby tugged at a strand of red yarn and began.

"One year, my grandmother came to us for Pesach. My grandmother was famous for her special Pesach nut cake, and we all looked forward to having her bake one for us."

"For hours and hours, my grandmother cracked nuts until she had a whole jar full of nuts for the cake. I loved nuts so much, that I decided to take just one or two. I was sure that no one would miss them."

Donny stared, open-mouthed. He just couldn't picture Bubby as a little girl doing something naughty.

"Well," Bubby continued, "I opened the jar and reached in. Just as I was about to pull out a handful of nuts, the kitchen door opened, and in walked my mother!

"I was so startled that I jumped backwards, pulling the jar with me. It crashed to the floor and smashed into thousands of tiny pieces."

Donny forgot to be shy.

"You did that, Bubby?" he asked, his voice squeaking in surprise.

Bubby laughed at Donny's surprised look and continued.

"My mother was very angry. She said I had to sit at the table and crack nuts until I filled a whole new jar for my grandmother."

"What did you do?" Donny asked anxiously.

Bubby threw a yellow ball of yarn on the bed before she answered.

"Well, I began cracking walnuts. I worked for what seemed like a very long time, and then I started to cry. My fingers hurt, and the bottom of the jar was barely covered. I could just imagine cracking nuts until I was an old lady!"

"Just like me," thought Donny.

"As I was just about to give up," said Bubby, "in walked my grandmother. When she saw my tear-stained face and the sack of unshelled nuts, she sat right down to help me."

"Just like you!" Donny said delightedly.

"Just like me. And do you know what my grandmother told me while we cracked the nuts?"

"What?" Donny asked eagerly.

"My grandmother told me that when she was a little girl, she had gone to her grandmother's house for a visit."

"Her grandmother had a big fat feather pillow in the living room. One morning, when my grandmother was bored, she poked a hole in the pillow and started pulling out feathers. When her grandmother walked in a while later, the whole room was covered with feathers."

"Just like the yarn!" Donny shouted.

"Just like the yarn!" Bubby laughed. "I couldn't imagine my grandmother ever doing something like that, but she said she did. Of course, her mother said she had to pick up all the feathers by herself. She tried, but it was too hard; she started to cry, and then guess who came to help her?"

"Her grandmother!" Donny cried out.

"Right again!" Bubby stood up and stretched.

Donny looked around the room. The bed was covered with neatly rolled balls of yarn, and the floor was clear.

"Come, Donny," said Bubby. "I think your mother kept dinner waiting for us."

"Finished already?" Mommy asked, as Donny and Bubby walked into the kitchen.

"Bubby helped me," Donny said, smiling as he thought of the generations of children who make mistakes, and their loving grandmothers who forgive them.

"Yes," said Bubby, as she spread out her napkin and passed one to Donny. "A little help from a grandmother goes a long way."

And Bubby and Donny shared a secret smile.